GREAT EXPECTATIONS

Retold by
William Bedford

Illustrated by David Cuzik

Contents

BOOK ONE

Being the first stage of
Pip's Great Expectations

CHAPTER ONE

The most vivid memory of my childhood took place on Christmas Eve when I was seven years old. I was alone and I was terrified.

I was visiting the graveyard where my family lie buried. There was my father, my mother Georgina, and my five little brothers in a neat row beside them. I don't know why I cried that afternoon. I had seen the graves often enough in my wandering games. Perhaps I was cold, or perhaps I was made sad by it being Christmas Eve, but I did cry, and I cried loudly.

Suddenly I stopped with a choked cry as the worst figure of my nightmares loomed before me. I thought he had come from one of the graves.

'Hold your noise!' the stranger growled, with a terrible snarl. 'Keep still, you little devil, or I'll cut your throat!'

He was a terrifying man, spattered with mud and trembling with the cold. He was all in coarse grey, with a great iron shackle on his leg. He limped and shivered, and his teeth chattered in his head as he seized me by the chin.

'Don't cut my throat, sir,' I pleaded, in terror. 'Pray don't do it, sir.'

'Tell us your name!' said the man.

'Pip, sir.'

'Show us where you live! Point out the place!'

I pointed to where our village lay a mile or more from the church. The man stared at me for a moment and then suddenly turned me upside down so that the church went spinning round my head and my pockets emptied. There was nothing in them but a piece of bread.

When I was the right way up again, I was seated on a high tombstone, trembling, while the man ate the bread ravenously.

'What fat cheeks you ha' got,' said the man, licking his lips and glaring at me. 'Darn me if I couldn't eat 'em.'

I begged him not to and clung on to my tombstone, trying not to cry.

'Now lookee here!' said the man. 'Where do ye live, supposin' I'm kind enough to let you live?'

'With my sister, sir – Mrs Gargery – wife of Joe Gargery, the blacksmith, sir.'

'Blacksmith, eh?' said he, and looked down at his leg. After looking darkly at his leg and me several times, he came closer to my tombstone, took me by both arms and suddenly tilted me back as far as he could hold me, peering all the time into my eyes.

'You know what a file is, boy?' he said, in his harsh, growling voice.

'Yes, sir.'

'You know what wittles is?'

'Yes, sir.'

He tilted me over a little more, making me go dizzy with helplessness and terror.

'You get me a file.' He tilted me again. 'And you get me wittles. You bring 'em both to me!' He gave me a tremendous shake, just to make sure I was listening. 'You fail, and your heart and your liver shall be tore out, roasted and ate,' he said. 'And don't you go thinking I'm alone. I ain't. There's a young man with me out on these marshes who will creep his way into a boy's room at night, and it don't matter how a boy hides, he will tear him open. Now, what do you say?'

'I'll get you a file!' I told him, in a mad rush of panic. 'And I'll get you what food I can, and I'll come to you early in the morning, I promise!'

'Say the Lord strike you dead if you don't!' said the man.

'The Lord strike me dead!' I cried, and I meant it too! He let go of my arms, leaving me free to jump down from my tombstone.

'Now,' he said, 'you remember what you've undertook, and you remember that young man who I told you of, and you get home!'

'G-good night, sir,' I called, nervously.

He was still shivering and he hugged his body in both his arms as I fled from the gloomy churchyard.

CHAPTER TWO

I ran all the way home, my heart racing like a frightened hare. When I got home, the forge was shut up, and Joe was sitting alone in the kitchen. He looked up anxiously the moment I burst in.

'Your sister has been out a dozen times, looking for you, Pip,' he said, urgently. 'She's out now, and what's worse, she's got Tickler with her.'

At these words, my spirits sank even more. I looked in great depression at the fire. Tickler was a wax-ended piece of cane, worn smooth by the frequent beatings my sister gave me, swinging her arm up and down with a tremendous force.

I glanced unhappily at Joe. He was a mild, good-natured, easy-going fellow, not at all like my rampaging sister. She had such red fiery skin I sometimes wondered whether she washed herself with a nutmeg-grater instead of soap.

I was wondering this when she threw the door wide open and, before I could hide, grabbed me by the hair and set about me with Tickler.

She was in a fine temper and took it all out on me. When she was satisfied, she threw me at Joe, who gladly settled me by his side near the fire.

'Where have you been?' she shouted, stamping her foot.

'I have only been to the churchyard,' said I, crying and rubbing myself to ease the pain.

'Churchyard!' sneered my sister. 'If it warn't for me you'd have been to the churchyard long ago and stayed there. It's bad enough to be a blacksmith's wife without me having to be your mother as well.'

Muttering angrily, she set herself to prepare the tea, hacking furiously at the bread. In our corner, Joe and I stayed quiet by the fire.

When the bread and butter came, and a mug of tea, we began to eat. But I knew I had to save some of my bread for the man on the marshes. I drank my tea and, when Joe wasn't looking, pushed my hunk of bread-and-butter down the leg of my trousers.

The wonder with which Joe stared at me when he saw my piece of bread gone was too evident to escape my sister's sharp eyes.

'What's the matter now?' said she, smartly, as she put down her cup with a clatter.

'Listen, old chap,' muttered Joe, shaking his head at me. 'You'll do yourself a mischief. You can't have chewed it, Pip.'

'Been bolting his food again, has he?' cried my sister. She made a dive at me and fished me up from the fireside by the hair, saying nothing more than the awful words, 'You come along and be dosed.'

Some medical beast must have invented Tarwater as a medicine, but I bet they never took it themselves. They wouldn't have inflicted it on me if they had. My sister kept a supply in the cupboard. With my head firmly under her arm, she poured a pint of Tarwater down my throat and then gave Joe a half-pint just for being under her feet.

It was a dreary Christmas Eve. I was hungry but made do with my tea, and at least I knew the bread was safely hidden. That was a relief, though I didn't feel really safe until I slipped away and hid my hunk of bread in my bedroom and then went back downstairs to keep warm by the fire. We stirred the Christmas pudding, and suddenly I heard a noise like guns.

'There's another convict off,' said Joe.

'What does that mean, Joe?' said I.

'Escaped, escaped,' snapped my sister.

'There was a convict off last night,' said Joe. 'And they fired warning of him. And now they're firing warning of another.'

'Who's firing?' I asked, infuriating my sister.

'Lord bless the boy!' she exclaimed. 'The Hulks! They're firing from the ships where the prisoners are kept, before they're transported from the marshes.'

'Why are people put into prison-ships?' I said aloud, thinking about the man in the churchyard.

It was too much for Mrs Joe, and I was hit around the head with her thimble and bundled off to bed without a candle. If I slept at all that night, it was only to imagine myself drifting down the river to the Hulks.

As soon as the grey of dawn flecked the sky, I crept downstairs. Every creaking board cried 'Stop thief!' In the pantry, I helped myself to bread and cheese, some brandy and a pork pie. From the forge, I stole a file. Then I ran for the misty marshes.

It was a cold and damp morning, and the mist was heavy and achingly cold. I saw the man sitting on the ground, but when I crept up behind him and touched his shoulder, he instantly jumped up. My heart stopped beating: it was not the same man!

He swore an oath and made a hit at me, but it was a weak blow and, as he stumbled away, I ran. 'It's the young man the convict told me about,' I thought, in my terror. If he caught me, he would tear my heart out and eat it!

I ran away as fast as I could and soon found the first convict, hugging himself and limping, waiting for me. He was shaking with the cold. His eyes looked wild with hunger.

'What's in the bottle, boy?' said he.

'Brandy,' said I.

He was already eating hungrily but left off to take some of the brandy. He shivered all the while.

'You brought no one with you?' he asked, desperately.

'No, sir!'

''Tis kind of you indeed to help someone in so wretched a state as myself,' said the convict, gruffly. He rubbed his ragged sleeve over his eyes to wipe away the tears.

'I am glad you're enjoying it,' I said.

'Thankee, my boy. I am.'

'I am afraid you won't leave any of it for him,' I said, timidly.

'Who's him?' said my friend, looking up quickly and stopping in his crunching of pie-crust.

'The young man you spoke of. I saw him.'

My convict's eyes widened. 'When?'

'Just now.'

'Where?'

'Over there,' said I, pointing. 'I thought it was you. He was dressed like you, you know,' I explained, trembling. 'And with the same reason for wanting a file,' I added, meaning the iron shackle on his leg.

'Where is he?' my friend said, cramming what little food was left into his jacket pocket.

I pointed in the direction the young man had gone, and he looked up at it for an instant. But then he was down on the wet grass, filing at his iron like a madman. I told him I must go, but he took no notice. I thought the best thing I could do was to slip off. The last I heard of him was the sound of the file rasping on the iron shackle.

CHAPTER THREE

I ate my Christmas dinner in dread, fearing that the theft would be discovered. We had friends with us from the village and Uncle Pumblechook from the nearby town.

We had come to the end of our first course when my sister said to Joe, 'Go and get clean plates', and I knew the theft of the food was about to be discovered. 'You must taste,' my sister went on, 'a delightful and delicious present from Uncle Pumblechook. A savoury pork pie.'

'You shall have some, Pip,' Joe whispered in my ear, but before he had finished his kindness my sister was back in the room.

'Thieves, burglars, vagabonds!' she shrieked, staring wildly around. 'The pork pie has been stolen!'

The tumult was tremendous. Everybody, except Joe, leapt to their feet and started shouting. In my terror, I felt that I could bear no more. I had hardly slept in the night, I had been frightened half to death on the marshes, and now I was to be found out as a thief.

I ran for my life.

But I got no further than the house door,

for there I ran head foremost into a party of soldiers, one of them holding out a pair of handcuffs. He was looking straight at me.

I thought I might faint at his feet, but the sergeant pushed his way into the kitchen and looked round cheerfully at the company.

'Excuse me, ladies and gentlemen,' he said, 'I am on a chase in the name of the king, and I want the blacksmith.'

'And what might you want with *him*?' retorted my sister, quick to resent Joe's being wanted at all.

What the sergeant wanted was somebody to mend a pair of handcuffs, and, while Joe inspected the damaged lock, the soldiers filled the kitchen with their noise, and the stolen food was forgotten. Joe got his coat and went off to the forge, and once the fire was blazing, began to hammer and clink, hammer and clink, while we all stood around and watched.

At last the handcuffs were repaired. Then Joe mustered his courage and suggested some of us might go along with the soldiers and see what came of the hunt.

'If you bring the boy back with his head blown to bits by a musket,' said my sister, 'don't look to me to put it together again.'

When we were all out in the raw night air and Joe had lifted me to his shoulders, I

whispered, 'I hope, Joe, we shan't find them.'
And Joe whispered to me, 'So do I, young Pip.'
Poor Joe! He did not realise that my own
wishes were entirely selfish.

And off we went, stumbling across the
damp marshes, losing our way and listening to
the shouts of the soldiers. It was hard to
imagine finding anybody on the marshes, and
my heart rose in the hope they might get away.

But we did find them. They were fighting
and splashing in the mud. Oaths were being
shouted and blows struck. In their eagerness to
hurt each other, they seemed not to care about
being caught. The soldiers went down into the
ditch and dragged them apart, my convict and
the other one.

'Listen,' shouted my convict, wiping blood from his face. 'I stopped him escaping! I gave him up to you!'

'It'll do you small good,' the sergeant said, 'you being in the same plight yourself. Handcuffs there!'

'I took him,' my convict said, with a greedy laugh, ignoring the sergeant. 'I took him, and he knows it. That's enough for me.'

They seemed about to start fighting again, but the sergeant gave his orders, and the convict I call the other one was marched off with his guard.

My convict never looked at me, except once, glancing at me as I clung to Joe's shoulders. Then, suddenly, he turned to the sergeant. 'I wish to say something about my escape,' he said. 'It may save some others laying under suspicion because of me.'

'You can say what you like,' returned the sergeant, impatient to be off.

'A man can't starve is what I want to say. I took some wittles, up at the village over yonder, where the church stands out on the marshes.'

'You mean you stole,' said the sergeant.

'And I'll tell you where from. From the blacksmith's. Some broken wittles, and a dram of brandy, and a pie.'

'Have you happened to miss a pie, blacksmith?' the sergeant asked.

'My wife did,' Joe exclaimed. 'Just as you arrived.'

'So,' said my convict, 'you're the blacksmith are you? Then I'm sorry to say, I've eat your pie.'

He never looked at me again and, with that, he was led away, across the marshes back to the Hulks.

My state of mind was eased, and I felt no need to admit my guilt to Joe. I loved Joe and feared losing his confidence if I admitted my crime.

When we got home there was great excitement, but I was too tired to listen and went straight to bed where I slept safe and without dreams.

CHAPTER FOUR

The winter months wore on without any more excitement, and then one night my sister sent me to the Three Jolly Bargemen with strict orders to bring Joe home. I found him happily smoking his pipe.

'Halloa, Pip, old chap!' he cried, and the moment he said my name a stranger in the bar turned his head and looked at me.

He was a secretive-looking man, his head held awkwardly on one side and one of his eyes half shut up as if from a fight. He looked at me hard all the time.

'You was saying', he said, 'that you was a blacksmith.'

'Yes. I am,' said Joe.

The stranger looked at me again. 'He's a likely young parcel of bones. What is it you call him?'

'Pip,' said Joe.

The stranger nodded and ordered rum-and-water. When it came, he stirred the drink not with a spoon but with a file – a file like the one I had stolen to help my convict. He did this so that nobody but I saw the file, then he put it back in a breast-pocket.

I knew instantly that he was sent by the convict on the marshes. In my panic, I told Joe we had to go home urgently, and we got up to go. I am sure my face was as red as the fire or as white as snow. I thought I might faint.

'Stop half a moment, Mr Gargery,' said the strange man, seeing us about to go. 'I think I've got a bright new shilling somewhere in my pocket, and if I have, the boy Pip shall have it.'

He folded the coin into some crumpled paper and gave it to me. 'Yours!' said he, looking hard into my eyes. 'Mind! Your own.'

My sister was not in a very bad temper when we returned home, and Joe told her about the silver shilling. 'A bad un, I'll be bound,' said Mrs Joe, triumphantly, 'or he wouldn't have give it to the boy. Let's look at it.'

I took it out of the paper, and it proved to be a good one. 'But what's this,' said Mrs Joe, throwing down the shilling and catching up the paper. 'Two one-pound notes!'

Nothing less than two fat one-pound notes!

Joe caught up his hat again and ran with them to the Jolly Bargemen, but the man was gone. My sister put them under a teapot on the mantelpiece, and there they remained, a nightmare to me, many and many a night and day, a reminder of what a terrible thing it was to be on secret terms with convicts.

CHAPTER FIVE

One day when I was nine years old we had news which brought fresh excitement.

I had been at my schooling, when my sister and Uncle Pumblechook returned from town.

'Now,' said Mrs Joe, 'if this boy ain't grateful this night, he never will be!'

'He will be, he will be,' beamed Uncle Pumblechook.

I stared at Joe. Joe stared at me.

'What are you staring at?' my sister cried. 'Is the house on fire?' Then she turned on me. 'You are to visit Miss Havisham!' she announced, in her snappish way.

I had heard of Miss Havisham – everybody had – an immensely rich and grim lady who lived in a dismal house.

'She wants this boy to go and play there. And he had better play there,' said my sister, shaking her head at me, 'or I'll work him.'

'I wonder how she comes to know Pip!' said Joe, astounded.

'Noodle!' cried my sister. 'Who said she knew him?'

'She doesn't know him!' said Joe, wide-eyed.

'No, she doesn't know him,' snapped my sister.

It seemed that Miss Havisham had asked Uncle Pumblechook if he knew of any boy who might like to go and play at her house.

'For all we know,' my sister went on, in her reproachful manner, 'this boy's fortune may be made by his going to Miss Havisham's. Uncle Pumblechook has offered to take him into town tonight and to take him with his own hands to Miss Havisham's tomorrow morning.'

And with that, she pounced upon me, and I was soaped, and thumped, and towelled and rasped and scrubbed until I was really quite beside myself. 'You ent a gentleman,' my sister told me, in her cross-tempered way, 'but you can be clean as a gentlemen.' When my scrubbing ordeal was over, I was put into clean linen and was ready to leave for town.

Nobody asked me what I thought. I spent a restless night at Uncle Pumblechook's, wondering in a confused sort of way why a rich stranger would ask to see me and getting nowhere with my wondering. I had never seen Miss Havisham and had no very clear idea how the rich lived, except that they didn't live like us at the forge. But I knew my sister was right. I was no gentleman, even if I was clean, and I couldn't imagine what Miss Havisham was going to make of me.

In the morning, we rang the bell at Miss Havisham's, and a young lady came to the gate. She was very pretty and seemed very proud.

'Come with me, boy,' she said, when Uncle Pumblechook had been sent away. She led me along dark passages and left me in darkness outside a door. I knocked and was told to enter.

I found myself in a large room lighted with wax candles. In an armchair sat the strangest lady I had ever seen. She was dressed all in white. Her shoes were white. She had a long white veil and bridal flowers in her hair, but her hair was white. She had not quite finished dressing for she had but one shoe on – the other was on the table near her hand. A handkerchief, gloves, flowers and a prayer book were heaped confusedly on the table. Everything was white, or had been white long ago, but had lost its colour and was faded and yellow.

I saw that the bride within the bridal dress had withered like her dress and flowers, and had no brightness left but the brightness of her sunken eyes. She had shrunk to skin and bone.

I should have cried out, but I could make no sound.

'Who is it?' Miss Havisham asked, sharply.

'Pip, ma'am.'

'Come nearer; let me look at you.' I went and stood before her, avoiding her eyes. 'Look at me,' said Miss Havisham. 'You are not afraid of a woman who has never seen the sun since you were born?'

'No,' I said. I lied.

She laid her hand on her heart. 'Do you know what I touch here?' she said.

'Your heart.'

'Broken!'

She uttered the word with a weird smile, as if she were boasting, then sighed. 'I am tired,' she said. 'Play! Play, play, play!'

For a moment, I had a desperate idea of riding round the room like a horse and trap, but I could not do it. I stood and looked at her, wondering what my sister would do when she found out about my disobedience.

Miss Havisham turned her eyes from me and sighed. 'Very well. Call Estella,' she said. 'You can do that?'

When the proud young lady returned, Miss Havisham told her to play cards with me.

'With this boy! Why, he is a common labouring-boy!'

'Well?' Miss Havisham said. 'You can break his heart, can't you!'

And so we played cards while Miss Havisham watched. We played 'Beggar My Neighbour'. I felt I was already a beggar and wished I wasn't – wouldn't it be grand to be a gentleman with these rich ladies. But Estella gave me no chance of such dreams. 'What coarse hands he has!' she said, while she dealt the cards. 'And what thick boots!'

She won the first game, and then I dealt. I misdealt, and she denounced me for a stupid, clumsy labouring-boy.

'You say nothing of her,' remarked Miss Havisham. 'What do you think of her?'

'I don't like to say.'

'Tell me in my ear,' said Miss Havisham.

'I think she is very proud.'

'Anything else?'

'I think she is very pretty.'

'Anything else?'

'I think I should like to go home.'

I was set free after more of this cruel play, and Estella brought me some bread and meat and a mug of beer. There were tears in my eyes. I ate the food and drank the beer and felt better when she came back.

As I was passing through the gate, she touched me with a taunting hand. 'Why don't you cry?'

'Because I don't want to.'

'You do,' said she. 'You have been crying, and you are near crying again now.'

She laughed and pushed me out of the gates, and I set off on the four-mile walk back to our forge.

When I got home, my sister was eager to know all about Miss Havisham, and soon Uncle Pumblechook joined her to bully the truth out of me. They so hounded and chased me with their questions that I invented the wildest things to make them leave me alone.

'She was sitting', I said, 'in a black velvet coach. And Estella handed her cake on a gold plate. And there were four dogs, and they fought for veal cutlets out of a silver basket.'

'And where was this coach?' asked my sister, in astonishment.

'In Miss Havisham's room,' I told them. 'And there were guns and flags and swords. But there weren't any horses.'

After Uncle Pumblechook had driven off, I sat quietly with Joe beside the fire and told him I had made it all up. Joe contemplated me in dismay. 'Pip, old chap! This won't do, old fellow! You mustn't tell lies.'

I cried then and said I was miserable, and that there had been a beautiful young lady at Miss Havisham's who had told me I was common.

Joe thought about all this most solemnly, staring into the fire. 'Well, Pip,' he said. 'If you can't get to be uncommon through going straight, you'll never get to do it through telling lies. So don't tell any more of them, Pip, and live well and die happy.'

'You are not angry with me, Joe?'

'No, old chap,' he smiled. 'But don't never do it no more.'

CHAPTER SIX

The next time I visited Miss Havisham, I could not help hoping that Estella would be more kindly, but she was as cold and haughty as on my first visit. She behaved almost as if we had never met, showing me to a different room. 'You are to go and stand there, boy, till you are wanted,' she said, and left me without another word.

I stood at the window, in a very uncomfortable state of mind, looking out. I noticed a clock in the outer wall of the house. It had stopped at twenty minutes to nine, and I remembered the clock in Miss Havisham's room had stopped at precisely the same time. Left alone with my own thoughts, I wondered whether this stopping of time would find me trapped in the house forever.

A bell rang at this moment and Estella returned. 'Now, boy!' she said haughtily, leading me away and along another dark passage. We had not gone far when she stopped so that I almost collided with her.

'Am I pretty?' she asked.

'Yes. I think you are very pretty.'

'Am I insulting?'

'Not so much so as you were last time,' said I.

'Oh, you don't think so!' she said, furiously.

'No, I don't.'

She stamped her foot at this and slapped my face as hard as she could. '*Now!*' said she. 'You little coarse monster, what do you think of me *now*? Why don't you cry again, you little wretch?'

'I don't want to cry,' I shouted back at her, though the tears in my eyes called me a liar.

I don't know what she should have said to this, because a gentleman suddenly appeared out of the gloom and stood looking down at us. He was a burly man with a dark complexion and sharp, suspicious eyes.

'What do we have here?' the gentleman asked.

'A boy,' said Estella.

'A boy!' he glowered, turning to me. 'How old are you, boy?'

'Nearly ten, sir.'

'How do you come here?'

'Miss Havisham sent for me, sir,' I explained.

'Well! Behave yourself. I have a pretty large experience of boys, and you're a bad set of fellows. Now mind!' said he, biting the side of his forefinger, 'you behave yourself!'

With those words, he released me, and we continued our way along the dark corridors. 'Who was that?' I asked Estella, in a whisper.

'Mr Jaggers,' she said, haughtily. 'He is Miss Havisham's lawyer so you had better believe what he says. He never says what he doesn't mean.'

We were soon in Miss Havisham's room, and I forgot all about Mr Jaggers. 'So!' Miss Havisham said, without being startled or surprised, 'the days have worn away, have they? Are you ready to play?'

'I don't think I am, ma'am,' I muttered.

'Are you willing to work then?' she said, after a moment's silence.

I agreed and she told me to wait in the room opposite hers. I crossed the staircase landing and entered a dark airless room from which the daylight was completely excluded. Candles lighted the chamber. A fire had been kindled in the damp grate, and the smoke hung in the room like a mist on the marshes.

Everything was covered with dust and mould. In the middle of the room was a long table with a tablecloth spread on it, as if a feast had been in preparation when the house and the clocks all stopped together. In the centre of the table was a white cake stand, overgrown with black fungus, heavily shrouded with cobwebs.

As I stared at this horrible sight, I saw
speckled-legged spiders with blotchy bodies
running underneath the cake stand and
running out from it. I heard mice too, rattling
behind the panels of the room. In the
fireplace, black beetles groped about in the
sooty hearth.

I was so fascinated by these crawling things
that I did not hear Miss Havisham join me in
the room. She stood at my side. 'This', she
said, pointing to the long table with her stick,

'is where I will be laid when I am dead.'

I shrank from her touch, but she would not let me go. 'What do you think that is,' she asked me, pointing with her stick, 'that, where those cobwebs are?'

'I can't guess what it is, ma'am.'

'It's a great cake. A wedding-cake. Mine!'

She looked all round the room in a glaring manner and then said, while her hand twitched my shoulder, 'Come, come, come! Walk me, walk me!'

She leaned on my shoulder, and I saw now what my work was to be. I was to walk Miss Havisham round and round the room. This seemed much more comfortable than any talking or playing cards, and I set to with a will until after a few moments she stopped for breath.

'This is my birthday, Pip,' she said.

I was going to wish her many happy returns when she lifted her stick and stabbed at the pile of cobwebs on the table. 'On this day of the year, long before you were born, this wedding feast was brought here. We have worn away together, this feast and I. The mice have gnawed at it, and sharper teeth than the teeth of mice have gnawed at me. When they lay me dead, in my bride's dress, it will be on this bride's table.'

Estella entered the room as Miss Havisham finished speaking. I remained quiet. Estella remained quiet too, both of us watching Miss Havisham. At length, Miss Havisham said it was time for me to leave, and I followed Estella down through the dark house and out into the dismal yard.

In the courtyard, Estella opened the gate. 'Come here!' she said, to my surprise. I stepped closer to her, expecting her to slap my face again. But she said, 'You may kiss me, if you like.'

I felt the colour rise to my cheeks, but I kissed her soft pale face as she turned it up to me. I would have given a great deal to kiss her again. But I felt that the kiss was given to the coarse common boy as a piece of money might have been, and that it was worth nothing.

CHAPTER SEVEN

Miss Havisham never explained why I was invited to the house. Alone in my room, I dreamed the hopeless dreams of boys: that I would become rich, that I would be a gentleman and talk on equal terms with Estella. I never spoke of these dreams. With whom could I share them?

The years went by and my bleak visits continued. Estella was always about, but she never told me I might kiss her again. Sometimes she would be cold and sometimes friendly. Sometimes she would tell me that she hated me. No matter what Estella said, my own feelings grew stronger all the time. I loved her. For all the tears she caused me, and all the times she hated me and called me common, I could do nothing to stop myself loving her.

'Break their hearts my pride and hope,' Miss Havisham would say to her, 'break their hearts and have no mercy!' I had no clear idea what her cruel words meant, but I knew they were meant for me.

'I think my heart is already broken,' I said to the lonely darkness of my bedroom at night, but I never said the words aloud to Estella.

Miss Havisham and I slowly got used to each other, and I began to imagine we might go on together like this forever. Time had indeed stopped in that dismal house, and it seemed to be stopping in my heart.

But then one day, when I was about fourteen years of age, Miss Havisham suddenly announced she wanted to talk to me. She asked me what I was going to be. I told her I was going to be apprenticed to Joe, I believed, and then I enlarged upon my secret ambitions, my desire of becoming a gentleman. Miss Havisham said nothing in reply. She said nothing and gave me no money and left me with my restless dreams.

We went on in this way for a long time, and I began to think she had forgotten our brief conversation, then one day she again stopped short as she and I were walking round the wedding table and said, 'You are growing tall, Pip!'

I could not deny it, though she said it as if growing tall were a deliberate fault. She was thoughtful for a while and then said, 'Tell me the name again of that blacksmith of yours.'

'Joe Gargery, ma'am.'

'Meaning the master you were to be apprenticed to?'

'Yes, Miss Havisham.'

'You had better be apprenticed at once.'

And with no more discussion it was arranged that Joe would come to visit.

And thus, all of a sudden, I was taken as apprentice to Joe. Miss Havisham was generous in paying for my apprenticeship. 'Pip has earned a financial reward,' she told Joe, 'and here it is. There are five-and-twenty guineas in this bag. There will be nothing more.'

Joe muttered that he did not expect anything more, but she still called him back and repeated that the payment was all I might expect.

Uncle Pumblechook and Mrs Joe could hardly credit such a lavish sum of money. 'I knew she would, I knew she would,' the gleeful Pumblechook beamed, as if he had planned the whole thing from the very beginning.

I was taken before the Justices and bound apprentice, and then the celebrations began with a dinner at the Blue Boar and the company of all our friends. I recall very little of that evening, except that I went to bed truly unhappy, knowing that I would never like Joe's trade. I had liked it once, but I had seen a new way of life now, and it had unsettled me forever.

CHAPTER EIGHT

It is a most miserable thing to feel ashamed of your home. I started my apprenticeship, working side by side with Joe, and all the time I thought of Estella.

It is true, home had never been a very pleasant place for me, because of my sister's temper and her violent use of Tickler. But Joe had made it as happy as he could, and I had spent more of my childhood in the forge than in the little cottage. It had always seemed to me that when I should at last roll up my sleeves and go into the forge, I should be happy.

But I was not. I used to stand about the churchyard on Sunday evenings when night was falling, comparing my life with the windy marsh view, thinking how flat and low and boring both were. I was dejected on the first day of my apprenticeship and remained so in the coming years. I am only grateful that I never said so to Joe.

One day, my mind full of Miss Havisham and Estella, I decided to speak to Joe. 'Joe,' said I, 'don't you think I ought to pay Miss Havisham a visit?'

'Well, Pip,' returned Joe, slowly considering. 'What for? She might think you expected something of her? And you heard what she told me, Pip? She called me back to say as that were all. ALL,' Joe repeated, very emphatically.

I had thought of that too, and it was very far from comforting, but I went on trying to show Joe that all might be well, and I was only going out of courtesy to thank her. In the end he agreed to give me a half-holiday off, so long as I promised never to go again if I found myself unwelcome.

When my sister heard that I was going to be given a half-holiday off, she seemed quite indignant.

'What's a boy like that going to do with a half-holiday off, if he gets it?' she stormed at Joe.

'Don't lose your temper,' said Joe.

But she did lose her temper and, before you could blow a candle out, she was rampaging at Joe like a thunderstorm sweeping across the marshes.

I thought I had brought enough trouble with my asking for a half-holiday off, so I got myself ready and set off for town that hour, leaving Joe hammering at a horse-shoe and my sister hammering at Joe.

My walk the four miles into town had a sad reward, for Estella was not there. 'She is abroad, Pip,' said Miss Havisham, 'she is becoming a fine lady. Far out of your reach, Pip. Prettier than ever. Admired by all who see her. Do you feel that you have lost her?'

My face must have shown my misery. She seemed to delight in my unhappiness and broke into such a disagreeable laugh that I was at a loss what to say.

She repented enough to say that I should come now and then, and I left with low spirits, to make my way home in the darkness. Beyond town, there was a heavy mist, but I hardly noticed it, trudging slowly back down the dismal lanes to my dismal future.

As I approached the forge, I started to run, alarmed at the commotion going on inside.

I rushed to the door, and there was a group of women in the kitchen. On the floor, lying without movement, was my sister. She had been found unconscious on the kitchen floor, an enormous bruise at the side of her head. She would never go on the rampage again.

A neighbour had seen my sister flying from the forge in a rage, shouting about half-holidays and slamming the cottage door behind her so that it shook like a jelly. In the kitchen, she had taken a fall in her flailing way and hit her head hard against the range. In one of her rampages, my sister had been the means of her own injury.

In the midst of all this fuss, Joe seemed like a lost creature. 'She were a fine figure of a woman, Pip,' he said to me, many times, the tears shining in his eyes. 'You know she were that, Pip, old fellow.'

I found myself feeling the same sorrow. My sister had never been over-kindly to me, and I didn't miss her rampaging and her furious tempers. But she was my sister, and she had raised me after her own fashion, and I could not help but feel sad to see the wreck she had become.

My sister lay very ill in bed. Her sight was disturbed and her memory. Her speech was unintelligible. A girl from the village came in to help. Biddy was a kind, good girl and soon became friendly with my sister, who was a surprisingly easy patient. Her temper was greatly improved, and soon she could not rest without Biddy around.

After all the long years of my childhood, a kind of peace descended on the old forge and cottage.

CHAPTER NINE

I was in the fourth dreary year of my apprenticeship, and fast approaching eighteen years of age, when I learned of my Great Expectations. I write those words calmly, yet even now they set my heart racing and my cheeks blushing with a fever of excitement. My Great Expectations, which changed my life completely and forever, and the lives of all those around me.

It happened like this.

On a Saturday night, Joe and I were sitting in the Three Jolly Bargemen enjoying our rest, when a stranger entered the public house. He did not recognise me, but I recognised him straight away. He was the man I had met on the stairs on the occasion of my second visit to Miss Havisham.

'I believe there is a blacksmith among you,' he said, 'by name of Joseph Gargery. Which is the man?'

'That's me,' said Joe.

The stranger came and sat down with us. 'You have an apprentice,' he said to Joe, 'commonly known as "Pip"? Is he here?'

'I am here!' I cried.

'I wish to have a private conference with you two,' said he. 'Perhaps we had better go to your home.'

It was in the front room that the stranger finally introduced himself. 'My name', he said, 'is Jaggers, and I am a lawyer in London. I am instructed to tell you, Pip, that you will come into a handsome property. Further, that you are to be brought up as a gentleman in London – in a word, as a young fellow with great expectations.'

My dream had come true. Miss Havisham was going to make my fortune on a grand scale!

'Now, Mr Pip,' pursued the lawyer. 'If you have any objection to this scheme, now is the time to mention it.'

My heart was beating so fast I could scarcely speak and stammered the words, 'I don't think so, sir.'

'I should think not!' said the lawyer. 'Now you are to understand, Mr Pip, that the name of your liberal benefactor remains a secret, until the person chooses to reveal it. If you have an objection to that, now is the time to mention it.'

'Oh, I have no objection, sir,' I said excitedly, longing to tell him of my dreams of becoming a gentleman. 'I have always longed for this moment.'

'Never mind what you have always longed for, Mr Pip,' Mr Jaggers retorted. 'Is there nothing you wish to ask me? Now is the moment!'

I thought of Miss Havisham, alone in her great gloomy house, all the time preparing to lift me out of my miserable way of life.

'Oh, sir,' I cried. 'Can you tell me something of Miss Havisham? I know so little, and she always seems so cold and difficult to talk to.'

Mr Jaggers raised his dark eyebrows. He seemed surprised, biting the side of his finger furiously. 'Miss Havisham!'

'I went to play there, sir, so many years.'

'I know you did,' he frowned, looking puzzled, then glared at the fire. 'Well, you know your own business, Mr Pip, if that is your only question. Miss Havisham was a spoilt child. Her mother died when she was a baby, and her father denied her nothing. He was a brewer, a country gentleman down in this part of the world.'

'But a gentleman may not keep a public-house, may he, sir?' said I.

'No,' Mr Jaggers said, brusquely, 'but a public-house may keep a gentleman. Mr Havisham was very rich and very proud. So was his daughter.'

I could imagine the young Miss Havisham proud and having a proud father, but then Mr Jaggers came to the cruel part of her story.

'She fell in love with a scoundrel, Mr Pip, who broke her heart and got great sums of money from her. Great sums of money often go with broken hearts. The marriage day was fixed, the wedding dresses bought, the wedding guests were invited. The day came but not the bridegroom. It was on that day that all the clocks in the house were stopped.'

'At twenty minutes to nine!' I exclaimed, remembering all the clocks in the house.

'At twenty minutes to nine,' Mr Jaggers agreed.

It was a sad story and reminded me of Estella. I hoped I would see her again before I left the town. I would have to go and say goodbye to Miss Havisham, whatever Mr Jaggers said about promises and secrecy.

I was to travel to London where I would be instructed by Mr Jaggers in the ways of being a gentleman. I had no objection to the plan, I assured the lawyer, as he bit into his finger and glared at me. In my excitement, I had no objections to anything.

The coming days were a whirl of preparations. I hardly noticed Joe's dumbfounded unhappiness or Biddy's quiet tears.

'Pip's a gentleman of fortune,' Joe explained to Biddy, and Biddy tried to tell my sister who nodded and smiled and understood nothing.

'But what does it mean, Pip?' Biddy asked me, in her kind, slow way. 'What are you going to be doing, being a gentleman of fortune?'

'I won't be *doing* anything, Biddy.' I laughed at her innocence. 'A gentleman doesn't do anything. I am to be well enough educated to hold my own with the best of gentlemen.'

'And can't you be a gentleman without that?' she asked, avoiding my eyes.

'No, Biddy!' I said, proudly, 'of course I can't.' I was far too grand in my good fortune to notice the sadness in her smile.

I visited town to inform Uncle Pumblechook. He was as sure as I that the source of my great expectations was Miss Havisham and took credit for bringing me there.

I took my farewells from Miss Havisham, but she had already heard my news from Mr Jaggers. 'And you are adopted by a rich person?' she said.

'Yes, Miss Havisham.'

'Not named?'

'No, Miss Havisham.'

'And Mr Jaggers is your guardian?'

'Yes, Miss Havisham.'

I could get no definite word from her and no word of Estella, and I left the town for my last evening at home. I was to leave our village at five in the morning, and, when the moment came, a great heaviness filled my heart, despite all my excitement at going.

I ate my hurried breakfast by the fire and then kissed my sister who was laughing and nodding and shaking in her usual chair, and kissed Biddy, and threw my arms around Joe's neck. Then I took my little case and walked out.

The last I saw of them was when I heard a scuffle behind me and saw Joe throwing an old horse-shoe after me for good fortune. I stopped to wave my hat, and dear old Joe waved his strong right arm above his head, crying huskily, 'God be with you!' and Biddy put her apron to her face.

I walked away, my eyes blinded by tears, and began my journey to London.

CHAPTER TEN

It was a year before I returned to the scenes of my childhood. A year in which I scarcely thought of home, and never wrote, and lost myself in my new life as a gentleman. And then one evening a letter dropped through my letterbox. It had a heavy black seal and border. It begged to inform me that Mrs J Gargery had departed this life, and it requested my attendance at the funeral the following Monday at three o'clock in the afternoon.

Having written to Joe, to offer consolation and to assure him that I should come to the funeral, I spent the following days in sorrow and memory. The figure of my sister in her chair by the kitchen fire haunted me night and day. I could hardly recall my sister with much tenderness, but I suppose there is a shock of regret when learning of a sudden death.

I went down early on the morning of the funeral and alighted at the Blue Boar in good time to walk over to the forge. Poor dear Joe was seated by the fire. When I bent down and said to him, 'Dear Joe, how are you?' he said, 'Pip, old chap, you know'd her when she were a fine figure of a —' and then broke off, unable to say more.

Biddy, looking very neat and modest in her
black dress, went quietly here and there and
was very helpful. Food had been prepared for
the funeral feast, and all of our friends were
there, including Uncle Pumblechook who
busily pressed my hand and whispered to those
present that he was the founder of my fortune.

It was a warm summer day. We walked across the marshes and went into the churchyard, close to the graves of my parents and five little brothers. And there my sister was laid quietly in the earth while the larks sang high above it, and the light wind strewed the graveyard with beautiful shadows of clouds and trees.

After the funeral feast, when all the guests had gone, I asked Joe if I might spend the night in my old room, and he was very much pleased by my asking. He changed into his working clothes and looked much more himself, pottering around the house and garden.

In the evening, when the shadows were closing in, I took the opportunity of talking with Biddy in the garden.

'I think you might have written to me about these sad matters, Biddy,' I said.

'Do you, Mr Pip?' said Biddy. 'I should have written if I had thought that.'

'I have not heard any details of my sister's death, Biddy.'

'They are very slight, poor thing. She had been in one of her bad states when she came out of it in the evening, just at teatime, and said quite plainly: "Joe." As she had never said any word for a long while, I ran and fetched Mr Gargery from the forge. She made him sit down close to her and wanted me to put her arms round his neck. So I put them round his neck, and she laid her head down on his shoulder quite content. She presently said "Joe" again, and once "Pardon", and once "Pip." And so she never lifted her head any more, and it was just an hour later when we laid her down on her bed and found she was gone.'

Biddy cried and the stars that were coming out were blurred by the tears in my own eyes.

'I suppose it will be difficult for you to remain here now, Biddy dear?' I said, after a moment.

'Oh! I can't do so, Mr Pip,' said Biddy, in a tone of regret. I am going to lodgings in the town. I hope we shall be able to take some care of Mr Gargery, until he settles down.'

'How are you going to live, Biddy?'

'I am going to try to get the place of mistress in the new village school,' she replied.

'I shall be often down here now, Biddy,' I said. 'I am not going to leave poor Joe alone.'

Biddy said never a single word.

'Biddy, don't you hear me?'

'Are you quite sure, then, that you WILL come to see him often?' asked Biddy, looking at me with a clear and honest eye.

'Oh dear me!' said I, as if giving up in despair of Biddy's nature. 'Don't say any more, if you please, Biddy. This shocks me very much.'

I turned and walked away then in my pride. I was in truth annoyed that she should think so low of me, but my annoyance was false because she saw deeper into my heart than I did myself. The only person I was deceiving was myself, but I could not face the truth I saw in her eyes.

Early in the morning, I was to go. Joe was already working in the forge. 'Good-bye, dear

Joe!' I said, shaking his hand. 'I shall be down soon, and often.'

'Never too soon, sir,' said Joe, as if we had become strangers, 'and never too often, Pip!'

Biddy was waiting for me at the kitchen door. 'Biddy,' said I, in my self-deceiving way, when I gave her my hand at parting, 'I am not angry, but I am hurt.'

'No, please don't be hurt,' she pleaded, 'let only me be hurt, if I have been ungenerous.'

Once more, my eyes were filled with tears as I walked away. But I was crying because I knew in my heart that Biddy was right. I would not come back.

BOOK TWO

Being the second stage of Pip's Great Expectations

CHAPTER ELEVEN

The years went by, as they have a habit of doing, and I settled down to my life as a gentleman. I found London a harsh city at first. I often walked in the bustling streets around Smithfield market, because Mr Jaggers had his offices nearby. I never got used to the filth and grime, which seemed to stick to me whenever I visited. I loved to watch the ships on the busy River Thames and walk through the dense London fogs. Every few months, and to my great joy, Estella visited town.

I was to be educated for my new life by doing nothing but doing it in luxury. My secret benefactor seemed to understand that being a gentleman meant having ample money to spend on lavish tastes. I had no need to work unless I wanted to. I did not want to. I had seen enough of work during my years in the forge. I bought clothes, and read books and went to the theatre. I had a fine time, and that was good enough for me.

And then, when I was three-and-twenty years of age and still no nearer to knowing the true identity of my benefactor, a great event, the turning point of my life, occurred.

It was bleak and wintry weather, and first of all I had a message from my guardian, Mr Jaggers. He wanted to see me in his offices. In the blustery, damp cold, I hurried through the grimy London streets, wondering why he needed to see me so urgently.

'Money, Mr Pip!' he greeted me. 'Do you know you owe money to all sorts of people?'

I knew it. My creditors gave me very little peace. In my early days in London, the idea had soon grown in my head that I must spend money to be a gentleman, and I had spent it. I soon developed expensive habits and began to spend amounts of money that would have seemed fabulous to me as a boy. I got on fast and enjoyed myself immensely. And my guardian was always there, knitting his brows and watching me with his suspicious eyes, waiting to see how I would turn out. This was not the first time Mr Jaggers had enjoyed my discomfort.

'How much do you think you owe?' he said, with his short barking laugh.

'I don't know, Mr Jaggers, at the moment.'

'Come!' retorted Mr Jaggers. 'How much? Fifty pounds?'

I shook my head.

'Oh, not nearly so much.'

'Five pounds?' said Mr Jaggers.

This was such a small sum that I blushed and said uncomfortably, 'Oh! more than that.'

'More than that, eh!' retorted Mr Jaggers, and so we went on until I had been forced to admit that twenty pounds would be enough for my present difficulties, and then the lawyer told his clerk to pay me the handsome sum.

This way of doing business had made a strong impression on me over the years and not an agreeable one. Mr Jaggers rarely laughed. He bit the side of his thumb and frowned his eyebrows together, and he always seemed to know more about what I was thinking than I knew myself.

It was not the first time he had paid off my debts, and I feared it would not be the last, but my unknown benefactor had always provided the money and, in my carelessness, I believed the money would always be there. After all these years, I still had no definite news as to who my benefactor was, but I believed my own suspicions and did not think Miss Havisham would abandon me.

But Mr Jaggers had not asked to see me solely to talk about money. Miss Havisham had sent a message from the country saying she wished to see me again.

'I can't think why,' Mr Jaggers said, 'but I am not paid to think why, I am paid to pass on the message, and I pass on the message. Miss Havisham wishes to see Mr Pip.'

'Estella may be back from Paris,' I said, speaking aloud my thoughts. I am sure my excitement showed in my face.

Mr Jaggers sniffed. 'She may. She has been seeing some wild fellow called Bentley Drummle. A very disagreeable, sulky fellow, and a bully by all accounts.'

'Surely not Estella!' I cried, in alarm. 'She would not be so careless with her happiness!'

Mr Jaggers turned his suspicious eyes on mine and bit the side of his thumb, waiting for me to calm down. My heart was racing. I had seen Estella often in the years since I left the cottage and the little forge, but she had been away for some months now. She was locked deep in my heart, where she had been indeed since the day I first saw her, and the thought of her needing my help made the colour rush to my cheeks.

'Sit down,' said Mr Jaggers.

'I have to go.'

'Go then,' he said, brusquely.

In my confusion, I turned to my guardian. 'I love her,' I said. 'I have always loved her.'

He would have had to be blind not to have noticed by now, but in his usual cautious way he would never admit it. 'I can't comment on that,' he frowned. 'I'm not paid to comment on that. You can't forget your feelings for her?'

'No. Impossible.'

'You can't try?'

'No. Impossible!' I repeated.

'Then you had better go,' Mr Jaggers said, sombrely, dismissing me with a sour smile. He had no time for talk about love, and I knew better than to try his patience.

I left his dismal offices and made my preparations to leave town immediately that afternoon.

CHAPTER TWELVE

I knew I must stay at Joe's and yet I could not. I had only been back once in all these years, for the funeral of my poor sister. Biddy had seen the truth on that sad occasion when she questioned my promise to return.

Now I persuaded myself that it would not be convenient, I was not expected, there would not be room at the cottage, and I should be too far from Miss Havisham's. I settled that I must go to the Blue Boar, and promised myself that I would visit Joe when I had seen Estella.

I was shown up to Miss Havisham's rooms as soon as I arrived. She was in her chair near the old table, in the old dress, with her eyes on the fire. Estella was sitting by her side, staring idly into the fire.

'Come in, Pip,' Miss Havisham said.

'I heard, Miss Havisham,' I said, 'that you wished me to come and see you, so I came directly. Hello, Estella.'

Estella lifted up her eyes and looked arrogantly at me. She seemed more beautiful than ever, with her fine Paris clothes and her cheeks warm from the fire.

Miss Havisham watched us with her keen

eyes. 'Do you find her much changed, Pip?' she asked.

I hardly knew how to answer. We had both changed over the years, but Estella only changed to grow more beautiful and deepen her hold on my heart.

Miss Havisham watched me with a cold eye, and when I failed to reply she turned to Estella. 'Is he changed?' she asked Estella, with a gleeful smile. 'Over the years, since you first saw him?'

'Very much,' said Estella, stifling a yawn and looking at me with her indifferent smile.

'Less coarse and common?' Miss Havisham teased, playing with Estella's hair. 'Less the blacksmith's boy, with the dirt of the forge on his fingers?'

Estella sighed and looked away. She seemed bored. She had grown harder as she had grown more beautiful, and I feared her hardness. It would bring her own ruin and unhappiness, as well as mine.

But Miss Havisham seemed irritated by Estella's indifference. 'Are you tired of me?' she demanded, suddenly, when Estella continued to stare into the fire. 'Are you bored with *my* company?'

Estella looked at her with her self-possessed smile, as she often looked at me. She showed no surprise at Miss Havisham's outburst, as though nothing anybody could do or say would ever move or surprise her.

'Bored?' she sighed. 'I don't understand what you mean. I am always bored.'

'You cold, cold heart!' Miss Havisham cried.

'What?' said Estella. 'Do you reproach me for being cold? You? I am what you have made me.'

'So proud!' moaned Miss Havisham, pushing away her grey hair with her hands.

'Who taught me to be proud!'

'So hard!'

'Who taught me to be hard!'

'But to be proud and hard to *me*!' Miss Havisham exclaimed, stretching out her arms to Estella.

I had never seen such passion or such disagreement between them. When Estella stood up and left the room, it was with a depressed heart that I followed her out into the moonlit gardens.

She treated me as a boy still, but she lured me on, knowing I loved her. We walked in the garden, and she told me she was going to London. I wondered if she was going to see the man my guardian had mentioned, Bentley Drummle, but I could not bring myself to say his name.

I reminded her of how she had come out of the house all those years ago and given me my meat and drink, like a dog waiting to be fed, and she said, 'I don't remember.'

'You let me kiss you once,' I reminded her.

'Did I?' she said, indifferently.

'Do you not remember that you made me cry?' said I.

'No,' she said, and shook her head and looked about her. I believe that her not remembering my tears and not minding in the least was as painful as the original crying.

'You ridiculous boy,' she said, playfully. 'Will you never take warning?'

'Of what?'

'Of me! I have no heart. You must know by now.'

'I cannot believe that!'

'Well you had better believe it.'

I knew then that I must speak. I must warn her of her own danger. 'Do you know a man called Bentley Drummle?' I asked, turning and facing her in the moonlight.

'What if I do?'

'Do you!' I demanded, angrily.

She gave me an icy smile. 'No!' she said, then turned away and walked back to the house. I was left alone with my thoughts in the wintry garden. I cursed myself for being a fool, but I could not control my heart.

I returned to Miss Havisham. She seemed to have recovered her ease of mind. When we were alone, she turned to me and said in a whisper, 'Is she beautiful, Pip, is she graceful and well-grown? Do you admire her?'

'Everybody must admire Estella, Miss Havisham,' I replied.

'But do *you* admire her, Pip?' she whispered.

'I always have.'

She drew me closer as she sat in her chair.

Her eyes were as intense as her voice. 'Love her, Pip. If she wounds you, love her. If she tears your heart to pieces, love her.'

Never had I seen her so passionate. I pulled away in my alarm, but she would not let me go. 'Love her, Pip!' she repeated, close to my ear. 'As I once loved someone myself.' I knew she was remembering her own doomed love. I made my excuses and left her as soon as I could.

I spent a sleepless night at the Blue Boar, knowing there was something low and mean in my keeping away from Joe. But, despite my promises to myself, I knew I would not visit the forge to see Joe or Biddy.

Over the years, I had spent many such nights, my conscience tortured by my ungracious behaviour towards Joe. In the dark weary hours in my rooms, I sometimes thought that I should have been happier and better if I had never seen Miss Havisham. Many time of an evening, when I sat alone looking at the fire, I thought, after all, there was no fire like the kitchen fire at home.

But, even now, despite these memories, I knew I would not visit them. I would leave in the morning without calling. There were tears in my eyes, but they soon dried, God forgive me, soon dried.

For even Joe could not keep Estella out of my mind. Far into the night, Miss Havisham's strange words sounded in my ears. Of course I loved Estella. I had always loved her and always would. But Estella did not love me. I could not understand Miss Havisham's cold cruelty.

I could not sleep for my unhappiness, yet little did I know what horrors awaited me back in London.

CHAPTER THIRTEEN

I was alone, back in London. It was a wretched night, stormy and wet, the wind rattling the windows. I had been reading for several hours when Saint Paul's struck the hour – eleven o'clock – and I set my book aside. I was listening to the moan of the wind when I heard a footstep on the stair.

Taking my lamp, I went out onto the stair-head. 'There is someone down there, is there not?' I called out.

'Yes,' said a voice from the darkness.

'What floor do you want?'

'The top. Mr Pip.'

'That is my name. What is the matter?'

'Nothing the matter,' returned the voice. And the man came on.

When he reached my landing, he stopped and peered at me in the gloom. Moving the lamp, I saw that he had long iron-grey hair and was about sixty.

'Do you wish to come in?' I asked.

'Yes,' he replied, 'I wish to come in, Master.'

When we stood in my room, I saw to my amazement that he was holding his hands out to me. Was he insane? Did he intend to rob me?

'Pray what is your business?' I asked, nervously.

'There's no one here?' he said, looking over my shoulder.

I shook my head in silence. I could not speak.

'You sure, Master?' he repeated, checking my other rooms.

Again, I shook my head. My mouth was dry

and my heart was pounding in my chest. I felt faint.

For I knew him! I could not recall a single feature, but I knew him! If the wind and rain had swept us back to the churchyard where we first met, I could not have known my convict more certainly than I knew him now. No need to take a file from his pocket and show it to me. No need to hug himself with both his arms and take a shivering turn across the room. I knew him!

He came back to where I stood and again held out both his hands. Not knowing what to do, I reluctantly gave him my hands. He grasped them heartily, raised them to his lips and kissed them.

'You acted noble, my boy,' said he. 'Noble, Pip! And I have never forgot it!' With amazement, I saw that his eyes were full of tears.

In my haste to see him gone, I turned to the tray where I kept my drinks. I found my voice at last. 'You are wet, and you look weary,' I said. 'Will you drink something before you go?'

He eyed me keenly, understanding the meaning of my impolite words. 'I think', he answered, 'that I *will* take a drink afore I go.'

As I filled our glasses, he watched me with the same intense watchfulness.

'How are you living?' I asked him.

'I've been a sheep farmer in Australia,' he said.

'I hope you have done well?'

'I've done wonderful well. I'm famous for it.'

'I am glad to hear it.'

'I hoped to hear you say so, my dear boy.'

I reminded him of the messenger he had sent to the Three Jolly Bargemen with the silver shilling wrapped in two one-pound notes, and offered to pay him back, but he shook his head good-humouredly.

'May I make so bold', he said, 'as to ask how *you* have done, dear boy, since you and me was out on them lone marshes together?'

I forced myself to tell him that I had been chosen to succeed to some property. That I had a guardian and great expectations.

'Some lawyer, maybe?' he said, with a smile. 'Taken on to act as guardian?'

'That's right,' I said, the first flickerings of horror moving in my mind.

'As to the first letter of that lawyer's name now,' he went on, enjoying himself tremendously. 'Would it be a J by any chance?'

Suddenly I knew the truth about my great expectations. I had to struggle for every breath I drew.

'Could it be that lawyer's name might be "Jaggers"?' he went on.

I could not have spoken one word, though

it had been to save my life. The room began to spin. He caught me, drew me to the sofa and bent on one knee before me.

'Yes, Pip, dear boy, I've made a gentleman on you! It's me wot has done it! I swore at that time, sure as ever I earned a guinea, that guinea should go to you. Lookee here, Pip. I'm your second father. You're my son – more to me than any son. I've put away money, only for you to spend. I've worked and built, only for you to prosper. But didn't you never think it might be me?'

'O no, no, no,' I returned. 'Never, never!'

'Well, you see, it *wos* me, and single-handed. Never a soul in it but my own self and Mr Jaggers.'

'Was there no one else?' I asked.

'No,' said he, with a glance of surprise. 'No one else. Who else should there be?'

I could not answer. The truth was too much for me to grasp. Miss Havisham's intentions towards me – all a mere dream. Estella – never intended for me. O Estella, Estella!

But the sharpest and deepest pain of all was that I had deserted Joe and Biddy. My sense of my own worthless conduct to the ones I should have loved the most was greater than any pain I thought I could bear.

I tried to collect my thoughts, but I was stunned. I stared into the fire, my mind reeling with all the dreams and hopes that had filled my life for years. All built on lies, or if not lies, then my own imagination, my own snobbish desires to be a gentleman!

'Where will you put me?' he asked presently, and in a trance I showed him to the spare room.

'You won't be having no visitors, will you?' he asked.

'No.'

'Because if I am caught back in this country, it would mean Death! I was transported for life. It's death to come back. I only come to see you, my boy, but I should be hanged if I am caught.'

'Hanged?' I gasped, trying to take in the dreadful word in my turmoil.

'Hanged!' he said, brusquely.

I realised a dreadful truth then. My convict had risked his life to return to England. He had risked his life, to see me. The knowledge was like a great weight on my heart.

I assured him there would be no visitors, and then I returned to the fire. I sat on the floor. My mind was in such confusion, I slipped into a restless sleep. When I awoke the clocks were striking five, the fire was dead, and the wind and rain were beating against the windows.

CHAPTER FOURTEEN

At first light, I went to find the watchman. I had resolved to tell him that my uncle had come to visit. Groping my way down the black staircase, I fell against something, and that something was a man crouching in a corner. He was gone before I could speak.

When I found the watchman, I told him about my visitor.

'Ah,' the watchman nodded. 'That would be the stranger who asked for you.'

'Yes,' I muttered. 'My uncle.'

'Likewise the person with him?'

'Person with him?' I repeated.

'I thought the person to be with him,' returned the watchman. 'They entered the building close together. Happen I was mistaken. It was a foggy old night.'

I returned to my rooms as my convict appeared. 'I do not even know by what name to call you,' I said. 'I have given out that you are my uncle.'

'That's it, dear boy! Call me uncle.'

'What is your real name?'

'Magwitch,' he answered, 'Abel Magwitch.'

'When you came in at the gate last night,' I said, 'had you any one with you?'

'With me? No, dear boy.'

'But there was some one there?'

'I hope not,' he said, giving his neck a jerk with his forefinger. 'I toldee it would mean Death. You think I was followed?'

'No,' I assured him. 'No, I'm sure not. The watchman was muddled by the storm.'

When we had breakfasted, I went out and secured lodgings in the name of my uncle. I thought he would be safer if he was living elsewhere and under a different name. After I had settled this, I told my unwanted guest to stay indoors and keep himself comfortable and out of sight, while I went off to see my guardian.

Mr Jaggers was at his desk.

'Now, Pip,' said he, as soon as he saw me, 'be careful.'

'I will, Mr Jaggers,' I said. 'I merely want to assure myself that what I have been told is true.'

Mr Jaggers nodded. 'But if you were told, then you were with the person. Perhaps you were informed?'

'I will say, informed, Mr Jaggers.'

'Good.'

'I have been informed by a person named Abel Magwitch that he is the benefactor so long unknown to me.'

'That is the man,' said Mr Jaggers. 'Abel Magwitch in New South Wales.'

'And only he?'

'And only he,' said Mr Jaggers.

'I always supposed it was Miss Havisham.'

'I am not at all responsible for that. I am not in the business of supposing.'

'And yet it looked so like it, sir,' I pleaded, with a downcast heart.

'No evidence for that, Pip,' said Mr Jaggers, shaking his head. 'Take nothing on its looks: take everything on evidence.'

'I have no more to say,' said I, with a sigh.

I made my dreary way home, where I found Abel Magwitch asleep by the fire. I sat down beside him, and, in my unhappiness, stared into the flames.

We talked into the dark hours, and we talked for several days to come as he told me more of his story. Each evening I took him back to his lodgings. I was never quite free from an uneasy memory of the man on the stairs, and I always looked about me when taking my guest out after dark, but I never saw anything to make me suspicious.

I seemed to slip into a desolate dream during that time, and my dream lasted for five days, until I came to my senses and knew that I had to speak to Mr Jaggers again.

CHAPTER FIFTEEN

'What is to be done?' I said, when we were safe together in his rooms.

'My poor dear Pip,' he replied, 'I am not paid to say what is to be done. I am only paid to say what has been done.'

'But he intends to go on lavishing money upon me,' I cried. 'I cannot bear it. Think what I owe him already! And then again, I am heavily in debt, very heavily for someone in my position.'

'Your position, Mr Pip?'

'Someone with no expectations!'

As soon as I said the words, they sounded strange and awful to me, having lived so long with my great expectations and very little else to keep me happy.

Mr Jaggers frowned. 'Why "no expectations"?' he asked.

'I can take no more money from him!'

'You are sure?'

'I am sure.'

Mr Jaggers looked thoughtful and paced up and down his room, glaring at the dusty floorboards. When he had frowned and grumbled to himself for some minutes, he turned and nodded his head firmly.

'The first and the main thing to be done', said Mr Jaggers, 'is to get him out of England. His life is at risk as long as he is here. That should be our first concern.'

'But he will not go, I know he will not go.'

'You will have to go with him, and then he will surely agree. His mind is all set on you, Pip. You can return to England once he is settled.'

'But how is that to be arranged?' I groaned.

'You must ask him,' said Mr Jaggers, 'when you sit at breakfast in the morning.'

With this plan formed, I left my guardian's office and went home to bed. I had the wildest dreams concerning Magwitch: of his being found and hanged as a returned convict. Waking, I never lost that fear.

He came round at the appointed time, and we sat down to our breakfast. I told him of Mr Jaggers's plan to get him out of the country to safety, and he seemed quite content.

'If you think that's best, my boy,' he said.

'Mr Jaggers does.'

'He is a clever man, Mr Jaggers.'

'Yes, he is. He has your interests in mind.'

'As long as my boy goes with me,' Magwitch nodded.

To drive the thought of the journey from my mind, I asked him about the fearful struggle he was having on the marshes when the soldiers found him. 'You remember?'

'Remember!' said he. 'I should think so!'

'Can you not tell me more about that man and about your own history? Surely this is a good time to tell me everything.'

And so Magwitch told me his story.

'Dear Pip,' he said. 'I'm not going to tell you all the details for it ain't a pretty story. In jail and out of jail, in jail and out of jail. There, you've got it. That's *my* life pretty much, down to such times as I got shipped off – after you showed such kindness to me.'

He had been brought up to a life of crime as a child, thieving turnips for his living, and sleeping rough in the fields and ditches. Then one summer he fell into the hands of a young gentleman called Compeyson.

'He were a bad lot,' said Magwitch. 'He'd been to a public boarding-school and had learning. He was a smooth one, that's for certain, and he knew the ways of gentlefolk, though he was no gentleman himself. He preyed off gentlefolk mostly.'

Compeyson set up the jobs they would do, the housebreaking and the burglaries, and Magwitch did the thieving. Compeyson had all the contacts to sell the things they stole. They went from bad to worse, the pair of them, and they were bound to be caught sooner or later.

'We wos caught red-handed by the Constables,' Magwitch growled. 'Me carrying one sack of valuables, Compeyson carrying the other. When it came to trial, Compeyson was all dressed up like a gentleman, and his lawyer blamed everything on me. Said I was a bad influence and had led Compeyson astray.'

'And they believed him?' I asked.

'Course they believed him. He looked the part and he played the part so they took him for the part.'

He glared with a ferocious anger into the fire, his hands twisting and grinding together, and I pitied any man who dared to cross him.

'And when the verdict come,' said Magwitch, 'wasn't it Compeyson who was recommended to mercy on account of good character and bad company, and giving up all the information he could about me, and wasn't it me as got never a word but Guilty?'

Compeyson was sentenced to seven years and Magwitch to fourteen. They were being transported to the prison Hulks when both made their escape, and Magwitch found his way to the churchyard. After that, when the soldiers found them out on the marshes, they were both punished with a fresh trial for escaping, but Compeyson got off lightly again. Magwitch's sentence was changed from fourteen years to life.

'Is he dead?' I asked, after a silence.
'Is who dead, dear boy?'
'Compeyson.'
'He hopes *I* am, if he's alive, you may be
sure of that,' Magwitch said, with a fierce look.
'I never heard no more of him.'

There seemed such violence in his words, I
couldn't speak, but looked in silence at
Magwitch as he stood by the fire.

CHAPTER SIXTEEN

The next day, I told Magwitch a mean lie: that I had promised to go down to see Joe. The truth was I wanted to see Miss Havisham. I left under that excuse and arrived at the dismal house, having sent a message ahead to Miss Havisham.

Why did Miss Havisham fill my mind during those dark days? My hopes of Estella were over, my dreams of our having a life together were ended. Yet I still felt that I needed to discover the truth: hear for myself that she had never intended us to be together.

I found Miss Havisham seated beside her fire and Estella on a cushion at her feet. I told them I had found out who my patron was. 'It is not a fortunate discovery,' I said. 'But it is a secret, and I cannot say more. I am as unhappy as you can ever have meant me to be.'

Miss Havisham looked at me steadily. Estella did not look up. 'Well?' Miss Havisham said.

'When I fell into the mistake of thinking you were my benefactor, you led me on,' I said.

'Yes, I let you go on.'

'Was that kind?'

'Kind?'

'Was it truthful?'

'Who am I,' cried Miss Havisham, striking her stick on the floor, 'who am I, for God's sake, that I should be *kind*? Who am I, that I should be *truthful*? You made your own snares. *I* never made them. What else?'

It was almost exactly what Jaggers had said. I had made my own snares, without any evidence. I had lain the traps for my own heart.

I stared unhappily into the fire before going on.

'I was generously paid for my attendance here,' I said, bitterly, 'and as you say, you are not to blame for my foolishness. But I have something I want to say to Estella.'

Miss Havisham nodded briefly and then turned her eyes to the fire, as if withdrawing into her own thoughts.

I looked directly to Estella.

'Estella, you know I love you. I have loved you long and dearly. I love you now.'

Without looking up, Estella spoke calmly.

'I have tried to warn you of this, now, have I not?'

'Yes,' I said, in a miserable manner.

'Yes. But you would not be warned, for you thought I did not mean it.'

'It is not in nature, Estella, to be so cold.'

'It is in my nature,' she replied.

I saw Miss Havisham look by turns at Estella and at me, but she did not speak.

'I must say what is on my mind,' I told Estella.

'Nobody is stopping you.'

'It is the same thing I asked you before,' I said. 'Is it not true, that a man called Bentley Drummle is pursuing you?'

'What if it is?'

'Mr Jaggers has told me he is a scoundrel and a bully and that he is determined to marry you.'

'So?'

'But is it true, Estella?' I insisted.

'It is quite true,' she replied, with indifference.

'You cannot love him, Estella!'

'What have I told you before? What have I always told you? I cannot love anyone. Do you still think, in spite of it, that I do not mean what I say?'

'You would never marry him, Estella?'

She looked towards Miss Havisham and then said, 'I am going to be married to him.'

I dropped my face into my hands, hardly able to control myself. When I raised my head again, there was a pitying look upon Miss Havisham's face.

'Estella, dearest Estella, do not let Miss Havisham lead you into this fatal step. Put me aside for ever, but do not throw yourself upon such a man.'

My earnestness awoke a wonder in Estella that seemed to touch her. She spoke to me in a gentler voice. 'I am going to be married to him. The wedding preparations are being made. I shall be married soon. It is my own act.'

'To fling yourself away upon a brute?'

But she would not listen. My bitter tears fell and she would not listen. 'O Estella!' I cried, 'how could I see you such a creature's wife?'

'Nonsense!' she returned. 'This will pass in no time. You will get me out of your thoughts in a week.'

How could she not know! She had been part of my existence since I first laid eyes on her. She had been in every line I had ever read, every scene I had ever viewed, every joy I had ever known. To the last hour of my life, she would be in my heart. How could she not know!

I returned home to London without further delay. When I arrived at the gate to my buildings, I found a note: 'PLEASE READ THIS, HERE.' I opened it. 'DON'T GO HOME.'

CHAPTER SEVENTEEN

The card was from my guardian and I quickly made my way to his offices.

'You had my message?' he said, promptly.

'Yes. I haven't been home. But what has happened? What about Magwitch? Is he safe?'

'He is safe. Answer me some questions, Mr Pip. You have heard of a man of bad character called Compeyson?'

My heart beat against my waistcoat. 'Yes. I hoped he was dead. Is he living?'

'Yes.'

'Is he in London?'

'Yes.'

I thought of the dark figure on the stairs, and the stranger the watchman had seen with Magwitch. Compeyson, alive and living in London. Compeyson, following Magwitch.

'Now,' Mr Jaggers said, 'questioning being over, there is business. Magwitch is taken away. He is living with a friend of mine down by the river.'

'Will he be safe?' I asked. 'Who is this friend?'

'Mr Pip, I'll tell you something. There is no place like a great city for hiding a person. I've hidden several over the years. He will be safe.

My friend was once a seagoing man. I did him a great favour in defending him in some trial. He lives by the river between Limehouse and Greenwich so that he can watch the ships sail up and down.'

'And Magwitch is safely there?'

'He is there. You, Mr Pip, must continue living in your rooms, to give the appearance that everything is normal.'

'The appearance?' I hesitated to ask.

'To anybody watching,' Mr Jaggers said, bluntly.

The next morning, I made my way to the address Mr Jaggers had given me, the Old Green Copper Rope-Walk between Limehouse and Greenwich. Throughout my journey, I kept stopping to see if I was being followed, but, if I was, they were too clever to be seen by me. I seemed to be alone.

I was shown into the little house and straight upstairs to where Magwitch was in comfortable hiding. There was a telescope at the window and sea charts on the table, and a bowl of fruit at Magwitch's side. He was seated by his fire, and I told him outright that I had come to discuss a plan of going down the river for a boat to get him abroad.

'So that I can be safe from Compeyson?'

'That's right.'

'I ain't frightened of Compeyson, dear boy.'

'No, but he might turn you in to the Constables. That sounds more his way.'

'And you are going with me, dear boy?' Magwitch asked.

'I am,' I replied, as Mr Jaggers and I had agreed.

And so we began our waiting. Most days, I took a boat and rowed down the river. I had not done such vigorous work since leaving the forge, and my arms ached with the effort, but I soon found my muscles growing and enjoyed the fresh air and the hunger that followed.

On rainy days, I sat with Magwitch by the window, watching the ships on the river, talking over our plans to get out of England. Mr Jaggers was busily and secretly trying to arrange a passage for our voyage.

The weeks went past. Whenever I went to see Magwitch, I checked the shadows behind me yet never saw anyone following. I rowed on the river, lost in my thoughts of escape, until I was a familiar sight among the watermen. Nobody took any notice.

My worldly affairs began to wear a gloomy appearance at this time, and I was pressed for money by more than one of my many creditors. I began to know the want of money and relieved the want by turning jewellery into cash. I had hardly enough money to pay my rent, but I refused to take further money from Magwitch, and he did not know of my plight.

I dined with Mr Jaggers, and he handed me a note from Miss Havisham, asking me to visit. In a few brief words, Miss Havisham told me that Estella was married. I folded the note and slipped it into my pocket. I could not hide the colour rising to my cheeks.

'So, Pip!' Mr Jaggers frowned, embarrassed by my upset. 'Our friend Drummle has played his cards. He has won the prize.'

I nodded bleakly, unable to reply. Mr Jaggers

watched me with his suspicious eyes. I might have been imagining things in my distress, but I thought I saw kindness in his eyes, sympathy in his awkwardness, though he would never have admitted to having such feelings.

'A lawyer has no business with feelings,' he had said to me once, in our early years. 'And feelings have no time for lawyers.'

With a heavy heart, I left Mr Jaggers and went back to my empty rooms. My mind was full of ghosts, dark shadows from the past. I hardly bothered to notice the shadows following me behind.

I went immediately to see Miss Havisham, having told Magwitch I would be away overnight. There was an air of utter loneliness upon her. She looked frail and very old, with her white hair and eyes worn with weeping.

'I have come,' I said, touching her hand.

She smiled, bleakly. 'Thank you, Pip. Do sit down.'

'Is there anything wrong, Miss Havisham?'

'I want to show you my heart is not all stone, Pip. Mr Jaggers tells me of your difficulties. I understand you owe money. I want to know, how can I help you?'

'You cannot, Miss Havisham.'

'Is there truly nothing I can do for you?'

'There is nothing,' I assured her.

She looked sadly into the fire. 'Are you very unhappy now, Pip?' she asked.

'I am far from happy, Miss Havisham, but there are causes other than Estella.'

'It is kind of you to say so. Is it true?'

'It is true.'

She seemed deeply moved. 'What have I done!' she cried. 'What have I done!'

'Very little,' I said, quietly. 'I should have loved Estella under any circumstances. You say in your note that she is married?'

'Yes.'

'To Bentley Drummle,' I said, almost to myself.

She did not hear me. 'What have I done!' she repeated, wringing her hands, pulling at her white hair.

I did not know how to answer or how to comfort her. I left her alone beside the fire and walked around the old town. My mind was heavy with grief, for Estella and all that had happened between us, for the troubles facing me now with my true benefactor. Every footstep I took was haunted by the past and a terrible future I could not imagine facing without Estella.

It was twilight when I returned to the sad old house. The mist seemed to have become thicker, but then I noticed the smoke in the cold air. Had someone lit a fire in the grounds? I glanced up to the windows of the house and suddenly I saw the flames. They were leaping from the windows of Miss Havisham's room. A dull red glow flickered in the darkness.

I ran up the stairs and threw open the door into Miss Havisham's room. She was on the floor beside the fire, struggling to get up. Flames from the fire were singeing her white dress and white hair. She tried to lift herself and cried out for help. I pulled my great-coat off and ran across the room, smothering the flames in the coat, dragging the cloth from the table for the same purpose.

When the flames were out, I dragged her from the room, shouting for the servants. One of them ran for a doctor. Miss Havisham was alive but badly burnt. My own hands were also burnt, but I couldn't think about that. Her white bridal dress that she had worn for so many long dreary years was, at last, destroyed.

I sat in the kitchen for an hour, shivering with sudden cold, drinking brandy to calm my nerves. I could not think about Miss Havisham without a heavy heart. She had been such a large part of my life, and yet her own life had been so bleak and wasted. Because of the cruelty of another, she had been bitter and cruel herself, and ended up alone. Even Estella seemed to have turned her back on Miss Havisham.

When the surgeon was done with his work, I went to see Miss Havisham, but she was in a deep sleep. I held her hand briefly and then left the room. I left instructions for the surgeon to contact Estella in Paris. Then I returned to London.

There was little for me to do now. Mr Jaggers was still trying to arrange a passage for Magwitch out of England. I spent my days on the river or talking to Magwitch in the little house. Magwitch talked to me fondly and seemed to like to have me with him. 'You are my good true boy, Pip,' he often told me. 'You ain't never let me down.' He seemed softened, and my heart softened with him. He was no longer the convict out on the cold marshes but an old man who needed my help. In all his generosity and loyalty, I began to see what a good friend he had always been to me.

And then at last Mr Jaggers sent me news.

CHAPTER EIGHTEEN

The day came for our adventure. It was one of those March days when the sun shines hot and the wind blows cold. I bundled Magwitch into the boat and stowed our bags, and at last we set out on our journey, rowing our way down the river.

'We be on our way, my boy,' Magwitch said. 'Faithful dear boy, well done! Thankee, thankee!'

'If all goes well,' said I, 'you will be perfectly free and safe again, within a few hours.'

'I hope so,' he said, drawing a long breath.

Night was falling fast by the time we reached our destination. I was all possessed by the idea that we were followed, but we saw no signs of pursuit on the river or the shore.

'Take a rest, Pip,' Magwitch said. 'We are in no danger, dear boy.'

'You are certain?'

'There's nobody about, Pip. Not a boat but ours on the river.'

'But we will keep a sharp lookout,' I warned, settling down for our wait.

We had been riding at anchor an hour before we saw the smoke of the steamer that was to take us across to the continent. She was coming towards us at great speed, sending waves rippling up the river. The sound of her paddles beat louder and louder. We got our two bags ready and I stood in the bows. For the first time, I began to feel the excitement of our escape. Magwitch leaned at the tiller, tired after the hard work of rowing.

'I said all was well, Pip,' he smiled, struggling to get to his feet. 'I said not to fret.'

As I turned to smile at him in my relief, I saw a four-oared galley shoot out from under the bank on the far side of the river and make rapidly towards us.

'Magwitch!' I cried.

'I see 'em, Pip,' he answered.

'The oars, the oars!'

'We can't make it, Pip, boy.'

'We must try!' I shouted in my panic.

But there was no time for us to take action. There was no escape. In less than a couple of minutes, the galley crossed our bows and pulled alongside. There were Constables in the galley and a shrouded figure sitting in the bows.

The shrouded figure stared at Magwitch, and Magwitch stared back. I heard him take a sharp breath.

'Compeyson!' he said, in a harsh, whispered voice.

'Compeyson,' I repeated, in my dismay. And I knew it was Compeyson. Even after all these years, I recognised the cruel face of the other convict I had seen that bitter morning on the marshes. Compeyson, come for his revenge.

Before we could say anything else, one of the Constables shouted from the stern of the galley.

'You have a returned prisoner there. That's the man, wrapped in the cloak. His name is Abel Magwitch. I apprehend that man and call upon him to surrender!'

At the same moment, with a sudden lurch of the tide, the galley ran into us, and there was great confusion in the darkness. I heard voices calling and men shouting. Our boat lurched violently to starboard and water flooded over the bulwarks. Magwitch was standing, and the figure in the bows of the galley reached for him, and then both men were in the water. They disappeared, grappling together in the blackness of the tide.

'Magwitch!' I shouted, leaning over the side of our boat. 'Magwitch!'

Then I lost my balance and stumbled into the freezing river to join him. I seemed to struggle with racing tides and flashing lights for an eternity and swallowed huge mouthfuls of cold dirty water, then I was dragged back into the galley by several pairs of hands. I saw our own boat floating away in the darkness.

We searched the waters and eventually saw one of the two men swimming towards us. It was Magwitch. He was dragged from the cold and sat shivering in the stern of the galley.

'No sign of the other?' one of the Constables muttered.

'Drowned,' Magwitch said, in a weak, shivering voice.

We pulled to shore and the officers formally apprehended Magwitch. He would be taken back to London as soon as a coach could be found. He was given warm clothing and a hot drink. His hands shook so much he could barely hold the mug.

While we waited, he told me he had been dragged under the keel of the galley and hurt his chest. His breathing was difficult and painful.

'This is all my fault,' I cried.

'Why you, dear boy?'

'It would not have happened if you had not come home for my sake.'

Magwitch smiled weakly and touched my arm. 'Dear boy,' he answered, 'I'm quite content to take my chance. I've seen my boy, and he can be a gentleman without me.'

Magwitch was taken to Newgate Prison and, after a brief trial at the Police Court, sentenced to death. Mr Jaggers did all he could to defend him, but he was a returned convict, and there was no escaping the awful judgement of the law. He was taken back to Newgate.

'The man who drowned was Compeyson, as you saw,' Mr Jaggers informed me. 'He followed you both and betrayed you to the Constables. He came along so that he could identify Magwitch.'

'If he hadn't been so desperate for revenge, he wouldn't have drowned,' I said, quietly.

'Revenge was not the man's only wickedness,' Jaggers said. 'You remember I told you of Miss Havisham's early years, how she fell in love with a scoundrel and lost her heart and a deal of her money?'

I stared at him breathlessly. 'Surely not?' I said. 'Not Compeyson?'

'Compeyson,' Mr Jaggers nodded firmly.

Suddenly, I understood all Miss Havisham's unkindness. An unkindness born of a heart broken by cruelty.

Mr Jaggers was watching me sadly. 'Revenge,' he said, darkly. 'That's always a bad business. And it breeds nothing but badness. But Miss Havisham is at rest, and Magwitch and Compeyson's long feuding hatred is over at last.'

Magwitch lay in prison very ill. He had broken two ribs, and they had wounded one of his lungs. He breathed with great pain and difficulty. I visited him every day.

'Always a good friend, Pip,' he said, in his quiet way. 'Always a noble friend to old Magwitch.'

His eyes were full of tears, like the night he first came to my rooms. But this time, so were mine.

The last time I saw him, he had grown much weaker. 'Dear boy,' he said, 'I thought you was late. But I know'd you couldn't be that.'

'It is just the time,' said I. 'I waited at the gate.'

'You always waits at the gate, don't you, dear boy?'

'Yes. Not to lose a moment of the time.'

'God bless you. You've never deserted me, dear boy.'

'Are you in much pain today?'

'I don't complain of none, dear Pip.'

'You never do complain.'

He had spoken his last words. He smiled, and I understood his touch to mean that he wished to lift my hand and lay it on his breast. I laid it there, and he smiled again and put both his hands upon it.

With a last faint effort, he raised my hand to his lips. Then he gently let it sink upon his breast again and passed away.

CHAPTER NINETEEN

I was busy for some days, attending Magwitch's funeral, talking to Mr Jaggers about my future. I had no money. Magwitch's estate was forfeit, because he was a returned criminal. All the wealth he had worked so hard to accumulate was lost. I had no inheritance.

Not long after the funeral, I was arrested for debt and became very ill. I was feverish for a long time and knew nothing of what happened to me. When I began to recover, I was in my own bed. Several weeks had passed.

I opened my eyes in the night and I saw in the great chair at the bedside, Joe.

I opened my eyes in the day and sitting on the window-seat, smoking his pipe, still I saw Joe.

At last, one day, I took courage and said, '*Is it Joe?*'

And the dear old voice answered, 'That it is, old chap.'

'Oh Joe, you break my heart! Don't be so good to me!'

'You and me was ever friends, Pip,' said Joe. 'Ever the best of pals. And when you're well enough – what larks!'

I had been ill a long time, and Joe had been with me all that time.

'What made you come, Joe?'

'It were Biddy said how Pip were not to be among strangers, but among friends. "Go to him," Biddy says, "he must not be left alone," she says.'

And so Joe looked after me, just as he had when I was a child, and we talked and remembered past times. It was Joe who told me that Miss Havisham had died.

'Did she linger long, Joe?'

'After you was took ill,' Joe said, 'she sort of gave up and passed away. She left her money mostly to Estella, the young lady whom you know.'

'I do,' I smiled, my eyes filling at the mention of Estella's name. But I did not burden Joe with the grief that name had caused me.

One morning, Joe seemed to have something on his mind he wanted to talk about. He was never any good at hiding his thoughts.

'Lookee here, Pip,' he said, in his thoughtful way. 'I know you got a soft heart and don't hold no grudges. But I often think how your sister used to lay into you with Tickler when she was on one of her rampages. You remember her rampages, Pip? You remember old Tickler, I reckon.'

'I do, Joe,' I smiled. 'But I don't think of that now.'

'Well I do, Pip, old pal. It were like this, you see, Pip, old fellow. When I was a boy, my old Dad used to lay into me and my mother something dreadful. He couldn't help himself, what with the drink and the temper he had. But he always had the stick close to hand, and if he couldn't find a stick, he used his fists.'

He sighed and shook his head, and I took his hand. 'It's not important now, Joe,' I said. 'It's all so long ago.'

'Things don't stop bothering a fellow just because they're long ago, Pip,' Joe said, in his slow serious way. 'I done what I could to keep you and Tickler apart, Pip. I done what I could to protect you when your sister was on one of her rampages. But my power were not always fully equal to my inclinations. She just beat you harder, Pip, if you follow my meaning. She just got hotter and beat you harder. When I tried to stop her, I only made it worse for you.'

'Dear Joe,' I said. 'Always the best of pals, dear Joe.'

'Always the best of pals, Pip old fellow,' Joe beamed, relieved to have got his troublesome thoughts out of the way. 'Always the best of pals.'

Our time together passed so slowly and yet seemed gone so soon. I woke one morning, when I was feeling much better, and found a letter. Biddy had been teaching Joe how to form his letters.

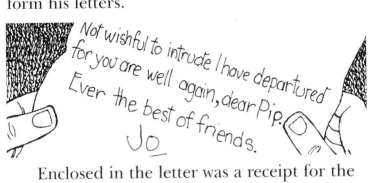

Not wishful to intrude I have departured for you are well again, dear Pip. Ever the best of friends. Jo

Enclosed in the letter was a receipt for the debts on which I had been arrested. I had never dreamed of Joe's having paid the money. But Joe had paid it, and the receipt was in his name.

What remained for me now but to follow him a few days later to the dear old forge, and when I arrived, I found him in his best suit, looking uncomfortable as ever and Biddy beside him in a new flowered dress.

'But dear Biddy, how smart you are!'

'Yes, dear Pip.'

'And Joe, how smart you are.'

'Yes, dear old Pip, old chap.'

I looked at both of them from one to the other and then Biddy cried, 'It's my wedding day, Pip, and I am married to Joe!'

CHAPTER TWENTY

I sold all I had and went out and joined a merchant company trading in the Far East. I became a clerk and eventually a partner in the enterprise. This was all done on the kind word of Mr Jaggers. When the owner returned to England, I was left in charge of our Eastern branch.

It was eleven years before I was to return to England. I was almost thirty-five years old. The counting-house in the East had been well established, and I came home to visit old scenes. Joe and Biddy had a child by now whom they named after me: another Pip, though blessed with happier times than mine.

In my restless mood, I visited the grounds of the old house where Miss Havisham had lived. The fire had brought all to ruin. Only ghosts moved in the ruins now. It was a sad, bleak place where so many of my dreams had started and come to grief.

I thought I was alone, but a stranger moved among the ruins. It was Estella.

I had heard news of her unhappy life. Bentley Drummle had used her ill, but he had died in a riding accident, and now she was alone.

'Estella!'

'I am greatly changed. I wonder you know me.'

The freshness of her beauty was indeed gone, but her voice was softened, her eyes were full of a kinder light. It was a light I had always known to be there. It was there when she was laughing. It was there in her moments of tenderness, however rare. She had been taught to be cruel, but her nature was not cruel.

'Do you often come back?' I asked, as we walked together.

'I have never been here since the fire.'

'Nor I.'

The moon began to rise, throwing its cold light upon us as we walked.

'I have often thought of you,' said Estella.

'Have you?'

'Of late, very often. There was a long time when I tried to forget how cruel I had been.'

'Cruel?'

'To you. I am glad we have met here, so that I can take leave of you more kindly.'

'Take leave again, Estella?'

'I hoped you could say you had forgiven me,' she said, quietly. 'I hoped you could tell me we are friends.'

'We are friends,' said I, pausing and taking her hand.

'And will continue friends apart,' said Estella.

I held her hand in mine, and we went out of the ruined place. The evening mists were rising now, and as we walked in the cold moonlight, I saw no shadow of another parting from my love. We would be married at last and leave the sadness of the past behind us.